THIS WALKER BOOK BELONGS TO:

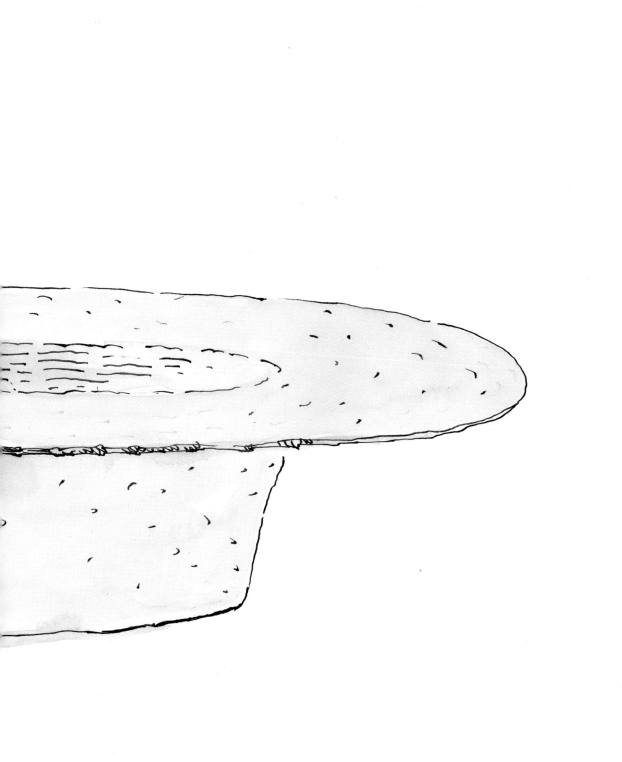

For Nathaniel
J.M.

For Richard
C.V.

First published 1986 by Walker Books Ltd
87 Vauxhall Walk, London SE11 5HJ

This edition published 1997

2 4 6 8 10 9 7 5 3

Text © 1986 Jan Mark
Illustrations © 1986 Charlotte Voake

This book has been typeset in New Baskerville

Printed in Hong Kong

British Library Cataloguing in Publication Data
A catalogue record for this book is
available from the British Library.

ISBN 0-7445-5245-1

FUR

WRITTEN BY

Jan Mark

ILLUSTRATED BY

Charlotte Voake

WALKER BOOKS

AND SUBSIDIARIES

LONDON • BOSTON • SYDNEY

Thin Kitty grew fat.

She made

a nest in my hat,

another in the

kitchen cupboard,

and a third

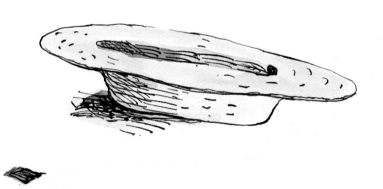

on Mum's skirt.

But she liked

the hat nest best.

All

night she purred.

And now my

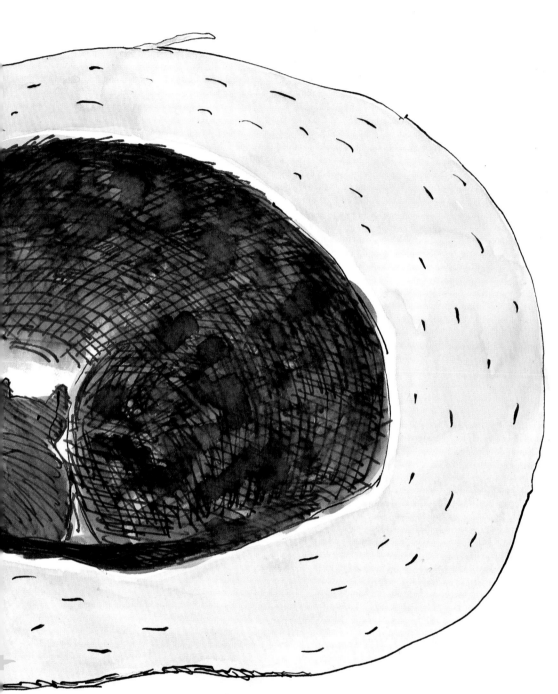

hat is full of fur.

Kittens!

MORE WALKER PAPERBACKS
For You to Enjoy

Also by Charlotte Voake

MRS GOOSE'S BABY

Shortlisted for the Best Book for Babies Award

There's something very strange about Mrs Goose's baby – but her
mother love is so great that she alone cannot see what it is!

"An ideal picture book for the youngest child."
The Good Book Guide

0-7445-4791-1   £4.99

TOM'S CAT

There are all sorts of noises around the house –
but which, if any, is coming from Tom's cat?

"Among my favourites ... ingenious and very funny."

Quentin Blake, The Independent

0-7445-5272-9   £4.99

MR DAVIES AND THE BABY

Mr Davies is a very determined little dog. He wants to go for a
walk with the baby – and nothing is going to stop him!

"Voake's attractive drawings turn Mr Davies into a hero and would
persuade the crossest mum to feel sympathy for him." *The Times*

0-7445-5237-0   £4.50